WRESTLING TROLLS

FUN & GAMES

Grab paper, pens, scissors, a friend
and complete the wrestling challenges!

BIG ROCK, PAPER SMASH, SCISSOR KICK

PLAY THIS HAND-TO-HAND COMBAT GAME WITH AN OPPONENT TO FIND THE ULTIMATE WRESTLING CHAMPION!

WRESTLING MOVES:

Big Rock: hand in a fist

Paper Smash: hand stretched flat, fingers together

Scissor Kick: hand with two fingers out like scissors

RULES:

Big Rock beats Scissor Kick

Scissor Kick beats Paper Smash

Paper Smash beats Big Rock

TO PLAY: Face your opponent.

Count 1, 2, 3 out loud.

On THREE, you both show your hand to reveal your wrestling move. Best of out three rounds takes the championship.

I'VE DONE THIS!

SUPER FAN BANNER

BIG
ROKK
ROOLS

Are you a Big Rock superfan? Create your own banner or placard to cheer him on. Use cardboard and coloured pens - you could even cut out a banner in the shape of Big Rock himself!

☐ I'VE DONE THIS!

TROLL TRUMPS

If you could transform into a troll, what would your troll be like? Create a profile card with your troll name, picture, strengths and signature move.

NAME:

STRENGTHS:

SIGNATURE MOVE:

☐ I'VE DONE THIS!

ROCKS ON THE MENU

ROUND 4

It's important for Wrestling Trolls to eat a lot to stay strong. Help Jack design a menu for Big Rock's day. Be inventive with your meal ideas, but remember the main ingredient: rocks.

EXAMPLE:

MENU

BREAKFAST:
Gravel cereal

LUNCH: Spicy pebbles on toast with sliced boulder topping

SNACK: Rocky road

☐ **I'VE DONE THIS!**

WINNER'S TROPHY

ROUND 5

The winner of the All-Comers Slamdown deserves an impressive trophy. Draw a magnificent medal or cup worthy of the winner - or model one out of clay!

☐ **I'VE DONE THIS!**

REIGNING WRESTLERS

Imagine you're in charge of the kingdom like Princess Ava. What rules would you make to keep everybody wrestling? What special wrestling equipment would you have in your castle?

Make a poster of rules or draw the plan of your castle.

☐ I'VE DONE THIS!

FAMILY TREE

We know about Milo's uncle Waldo, but what about Big Rock's family? Draw a family tree for Big Rock with all of his troll relatives - give them scary names and draw pictures to show how terrifying they are.

☐ I'VE DONE THIS!

BATTLE TROLLS

WRESTLE TROLLS WITH A FRIEND IN THIS PEN-AND-PAPER GAME

Copy out a grid like this with ten boxes across and ten down - two for each player. (Or you can use graph paper!)

Label one grid for your team name, and the other for your opponent's team name.

Choose the position of your wrestlers by filling in squares for each team member. Each team has three players of different sizes:

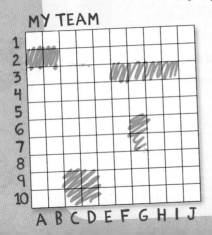

1 x Wrestling Troll:
Four spaces in a square

1 x Wrestling Orc:
Four spaces in a row

2 x Wrestling Goblins:
Two spaces in a row

TO PLAY:

Take turns to wrestle by calling out positions on the grid (e.g., 'C6!').

If your opponent names a space where you have a wrestler, call, 'pinfall!'.

If your opponent names a space when there are no wrestlers, call 'miss'.

Mark all your moves on your grid for the other team (so you don't call the same position twice).

Mark your opponent's moves on your own team's grid: a cross for a pinfall and a circle for a miss.

When all of a player's squares have been called, the player is knocked out.

The winner is the first one to knock out all the opponent's wrestlers.

MY TEAM

MY FRIEND'S TEAM

☐ I'VE DONE THIS!

WRESTLING RING

Had fun with these
games and want more
Wrestling Trolls action?

There's more fun and games
waiting for you right now on
www.wrestlingtrolls.com,
with free finger puppets to collect
of your favourite characters!

Join the Wrestling Ring and get a
free puppet of Big Rock to battle
with. Plus, upload your creations
from this section and you can
also earn yourself other
exclusive character puppets.

Log on now to
www.wrestlingtrolls.com

WRESTLING TROLLS
TO THE RESCUE

Chapter 1

The caravan with wwt on it creaked as it moved slowly along the country road. In front, pulling the caravan, plodded the old shaggy horse, Robin. Big Rock, the Wrestling Troll, ran behind the caravan, overtook it, ran round it, ran backwards, and then ran round the caravan again, all the time throwing punches at the empty air. He was training.

In the driving seat of the caravan sat Milo and Jack. Milo held the horse's reins and sang:

'Wrestling Trolls.
Tum-di-dum!
Wrestling Trolls.
Tum-di-dum!'

Milo turned to the glum-looking Jack and said, 'Come on! Join in the song! It'll make you feel good!'

'Nothing will make me feel good!' groaned Jack. 'I turned into a Wrestling Troll!' Hastily he added, so as not to upset Big Rock, 'Not that there's anything wrong with trolls, I love Wrestling Trolls. I just don't understand why

it happened. It's weird, and I'm worried it'll happen again.'

'So what?' said Milo. 'It was lucky for us it happened. You saved us!'

'Yes, but I don't know if it'll happen again!' He let out another sigh. 'Anyway, I don't know the words to the song.'

'There aren't any words,' said Milo. 'Well, there are, but that's all of them:

> 'Wrestling Trolls.
> 'Tum-di-dum!
> 'Wrestling Trolls.
> 'Tum-di-dum!

'And you just keep singing it over and over.'

'Until the poor creature pulling the caravan can't stand it any more,' grumbled Robin.

'It's a good song!' defended Milo. 'My uncle Waldo wrote it!'

'How can you claim he wrote it,' demanded Robin, 'when the only words in it are: Wrestling Trolls. Tum-di-dum!? That's not writing a song, that's . . .' The old horse struggled to find the right words and finally came up with: 'Stupid.'

'It's not stupid!' said Milo. 'It's a good song because everyone can sing it!'

'Trolls sang it when we had lots of trolls,' agreed Big Rock as he ran past. 'It good song!'

Then he disappeared again, running backwards.

Milo gave Jack a cheerful smile. 'So, what do you think we should call you?' he asked.

Jack looked at him with a puzzled frown. 'Jack,' he said. 'That's my name.'

'I mean when you're . . . you know . . . the other you. The big one. The . . . er . . .'

'Troll,' said Jack, and sighed again.

'Yes,' nodded Milo. 'When you're . . . him.'

'How about Thud?' suggested the horse.

'Thud?' asked Milo.

'It was the sound that door made as it came off its hinges,' said Robin. 'And so did Lord Veto's orcs when they hit the floor.'

'I like it,' said Milo. 'It has a good ring to it. Perfect for a Wrestling Troll.'

'But I'm not a Wrestling Troll,' said Jack. 'I'm

Jack. I'm a boy.'

'And that's a perfect name for you when you're a boy,' nodded Milo. 'But when you're . . . him. That big, tough, troll-like guy. He looks and sounds to me like Thud.'

'He certainly did when we were in those dungeons,' added Robin. He chuckled. 'Thud. Biff. Bash. And Thud again.'

'Excellent,' smiled Milo. 'That's you. You're Thud.'

'I'm not!' insisted Jack. 'I bet it won't ever happen again.'

'It'd be great if it did,' said Milo. 'Big Rock and Thud. Two Wrestling Trolls!' He frowned. 'I wonder what caused it? Have you ever seen anything like that before, Big Rock?'

'No,' said Big Rock, and he danced past them, throwing punches and kicks at the air as he went.

'What about you, Robin? You're a horse who's seen a lot. Especially with Wrestling Trolls.'

Robin frowned. 'I'll think about it,' he said.

'Right now, I'm going to stop talking because we have a hill coming up, and I need my breath to haul this heavy caravan up it.'

'We could always get off and make it lighter,' said Milo.

'That is a very good idea,' said Robin.

'And while we're off, I could always fix us a quick snack to give you energy,' suggested Jack.

Robin stopped, and if a horse could have been said to smile, then Robin was smiling. 'That,' he said, 'is an even better idea!'

Chapter 2

Lunch for Milo, Robin and Jack was a pie, made by Jack. Big Rock munched on a selection of tiny stones of different shades and colours, now and then taking a bigger bite out of a chunk of granite.

After lunch, the gang packed up and set off, with Big Rock once again running backwards and forwards around the caravan.

'Where's this place we're going to?' asked Jack.

'It's a town called Weevil,' said Milo.

'Has it got good wrestling?' asked Jack.

'Of course it has!' said Milo. 'Remember that special VIP guest at the Trolls versus Orcs Slamdown last week?'

'Princess Ava,' nodded Jack, remembering the small girl who'd been in the royal box.

'That's her,' said Milo. 'Well, Weevil is her kingdom. She loves wrestling. Her father, the old king, loved wrestling as well.' He smiled. 'I came here years ago with my uncle Waldo and the Wrestling Trolls, and it was great!'

'Good wrestling,' agreed Big Rock as he ran past, punching the air with his enormous fists.

By now they had reached the outskirts of the small town, and the wheels of the caravan left the dust of the earth road and began to rattle over the cobbles of the streets. The place looked pretty deserted, just a few people hurrying by, and all of them keeping their eyes down towards the ground. They trundled on through the cobbled streets until they reached the market square in the town centre. As in the rest of the town, only a few people were in the square, and none of them were hanging about.

'Strange,' muttered Milo. 'When we were here before this place was really busy. Loads of people. I wonder where everyone is?'

Big Rock pointed to a large building at one side of the square. 'That where wrestling was last time,' he said.

'Yes,' said Milo.

Now they saw that the doors of the building had been nailed shut, and there was a large closed sign placed over them.

'Strange,' murmured Milo again.

He saw a woman walking along, accompanied by three small children aged from about eight

down to just three years old.

'Excuse me!' called Milo.

The woman stopped and looked at him and the caravan and especially Big Rock with suspicion.

'Yes?' she asked.

'We're looking for the wrestling tournament –'

He didn't get a chance to finish. The woman uttered a shocked gasp and put her hands over the ears of her youngest child. The middle child pointed an accusing finger at Milo and shouted, 'Bad men! Bad men!'

'Hush!' said his mother, and swept her children away as fast as she could.

Milo turned to Jack. 'What did I say?' he demanded, bewildered.

'You said the "w" word,' muttered a voice.

They turned and saw that a man had appeared by the caravan. He was tall and powerful-looking with a battered face, and that face had a very unhappy expression.

'What do you mean?' asked Jack. 'Wrest—'

'Sssh!' snapped the man, and he looked

around nervously. When he was satisfied that there was no one else around to overhear, he turned back to Milo, Jack, Big Rock and Robin. 'You must be strangers here.'

'Well, yes,' admitted Milo, 'but I came here years ago with my uncle Waldo.' He gestured at Big Rock. 'With Big Rock here, and my uncle's other Wrestling Trolls.'

'Don't say that word!' said the man warningly.

'Trolls?' queried Big Rock, puzzled.

'I think he means the other word, Big Rock,' murmured Jack. 'The "w" one.'

'Exactly,' nodded the man. 'Everything about it is banned here. The sport itself. And worse, anyone who looks like a . . .' and here he dropped his voice to a whisper: 'wrestler, or is thought of as having anything to do with wrestling, gets arrested and locked up.'

'Why?' asked Milo, still looking bewildered. 'When we were last here everyone loved w— . . . it.'

'Yes, they did,' said the man. 'I used to be a . . . sportsman myself.' He pointed at his battered face. 'Which is where I got this face.'

'It good face,' said Big Rock.

'Not any more,' sighed the man. 'Because I look like a . . . sportsman . . . the townsfolk treat me with suspicion.' He looked gloomy. 'I've thought of moving to somewhere else, where . . . sport . . . is still allowed.' He sighed unhappily again. 'But I was born here. I like this town. It was a great and happy town until

General Pepper took over last week.' He shook his head sadly. 'Just one week, and this whole place has become a nightmare to live in!'

'A week?!' echoed Milo, shocked.

'Who's General Pepper?' asked Jack.

'He's Princess Ava's uncle,' said the man.

'But she was guest of honour at the last wrest— er, sporting tournament,' said Milo. 'I thought she loved wrest— er . . . sports?'

'She does,' nodded the man. 'She's absolutely mad on it. That was one of the reasons for the row between her and her uncle. He hates it, but she wanted to set up a school for . . . wrestlers. But General Pepper didn't want her spending any money on it, so when she came back from that . . . sporting tournament . . . he had her locked up at the top of a tall tower, and then took over as ruler of the region.'

'How did he get away with that?' asked Jack. 'Didn't anyone object? Wasn't Princess Ava popular?'

'Princess Ava was very popular,' said the man. 'When she was locked up some people talked about breaking Princess Ava out of her prison and overthrowing General Pepper. Especially those people who liked . . . sports. But that was before the General's soldiers went into action. And there are lots of them, heavily armed, enforcing the General's new laws banning . . . sports . . . and everything and everyone to do with it.'

'That's terrible!' said Jack.

Suddenly they heard a shout, and turned to see a troop of ten soldiers, all armed with spears, approaching. At their front was their leader, carrying a sword and wearing a captain's armour.

'You lot!' called the Captain. 'We've had complaints about you! We have reason to believe that you are involved in the criminal act of wrestling!'

Chapter 3

Milo looked at the Captain and the armed soldiers and laughed out loud.

'Us?' he chuckled. 'Good heavens, no! Nothing to do with us!'

'Then why did you ask where the wrestling tournament was?' demanded the Captain.

Jack and Milo noticed that the woman and her children they'd talked to earlier were now standing just behind the soldiers, watching them. Jack also noticed that the big man they'd been talking to had slipped quietly away.

'Well?' demanded the Captain accusingly. 'Did you ask where the wrestling was?'

'Er . . .' began Milo.

'Yes he did!' called out the little boy. 'Bad

men! Bad men!'

'No, we're not bad men,' said Milo. 'We're after bad men. We're bounty hunters. We catch wrestlers and bring them to justice. We heard that wrestling was against the law here, so we thought we'd find out where the wrestlers were, arrest them, and bring them to General Pepper and get a bounty.'

The Captain looked at Milo suspiciously. Then at Jack, and Robin, and finally at Big Rock. 'That troll looks like a wrestler to me,' he snapped. 'A Wrestling Troll.'

'No, no!' said Milo quickly. 'He's . . . He's a bounty hunter. We knew the people we'd be up against would be big and tough, so we had to find someone just as big and tough. That's Big Rock, the bounty hunter.'

The Captain regarded Milo and Big Rock suspiciously. Then he said, 'We don't want bounty hunters in this town. We keep the law here. Me and my men. You'd better leave.'

'We will,' nodded Milo. 'We'll be on our way immediately.'

'We can't,' put in Jack. He pointed at Robin. 'Our horse is very old. He needs to rest before we can move on.'

As if to emphasise this point, Robin let out a long and weary groan and sank to his knees.

'See?' said Jack.

The Captain looked at Robin, then nodded. 'All right,' he said reluctantly. 'But you leave town first thing in the morning.'

With that, the Captain turned, barked an

order at the soldiers, and they marched away.

'What are you doing?' demanded Milo to Jack, annoyed. 'We need to get out of here now!'

'We can't,' said Jack, his tone serious.

'Yes we can!' retorted Milo.

Suddenly they noticed that the large man with the battered face had reappeared.

'See?' said the large man. 'That was Captain Oz, General Pepper's right-hand man. As long as they're in charge, this is going to be a terrible town.'

'Who are you?' asked Milo. 'And where did you disappear to?'

'My name's Sam Dent,' said the man.

'Sam Dent!' said Big Rock, and he looked at the man with new awe and respect. 'Famous Sam Dent! Great wrestler!'

'Not any more,' said Sam Dent ruefully.

'You know what we have to do,' said Jack determinedly.

'Yes,' said Milo. 'Leave town.'

'No,' said Jack. 'We have to rescue Princess

Ava. That's why Robin and I pulled that stunt about him being tired so we could stay.'

'No,' said Robin. 'I really am tired.'

'It won't be easy,' said Sam. 'There are armed soldiers guarding the entrance to the tower to make sure that no one can get in.'

'That shouldn't stop us!' insisted Jack. 'Once Princess Ava is out of prison, I bet you the people will unite behind her. And then she can banish General Pepper and his soldiers into exile. And then there'll be wrestling here again, as there ought to be.'

'No!' said Milo firmly. 'It's too dangerous. We'll be putting ourselves at risk against a load of armed soldiers, all for a Princess we've never seen.'

'We did see her,' said Jack. 'She was in the royal box at that tournament at Lord Veto's. She was the guest of honour.'

'I don't care,' said Milo. 'We don't know her personally. I say we leave as soon as we've rested up for the night.'

'No,' said Big Rock.

Milo and Jack looked at the big troll.

'What?' asked Milo.

'Jack right. Girl in trouble,' said Big Rock. 'Bad man in charge here. Ban wrestling. We rescue girl, like Jack say. Bring wrestling back.'

Milo let out a long sigh. 'Look, Big Rock, it's not that I'm unsympathetic to this Princess, and obviously I will always fight for the freedom to wrestle, but –'

'You're scared,' said Robin.

'No,' said Milo. 'I'm just being careful about our safety. Big Rock, Jack, Robin, you're all my responsibility . . .'

'We rescue girl,' said Big Rock firmly.

'. . . and, as I'm in charge of this outfit . . .' continued Milo.

'Me and Big Rock will rescue the Princess,' said Jack.

'I'll help,' offered Sam Dent.

'And me,' said Robin.

Milo stopped and looked at them all. Then he gave a shrug.

'Yes,' he said. 'That's what I was about to say.'

Chapter 4

'We won't be able to rescue the Princess easily with just us against all these soldiers,' pointed out Jack. 'We need a plan.'

They all fell silent and looked at one another questioningly.

'Don't look at me,' shrugged Robin. 'I'm just a horse.'

'Maybe we can use the General's new law as part of our plan,' Milo said.

'How?' asked Sam.

'What we need are two wrestlers,' said Milo. 'They start a wrestling match in the town square. That'll bring all the townspeople in to see it, and all the guards will come in to stop it. And, while that's going on and everyone's attention is on the match, Jack and me get into the tower and rescue the Princess!'

'That brilliant!' said Big Rock. Then he frowned. 'But who do wrestling match?'

'Well, as Jack and I will be in the tower rescuing the Princess, and as Robin can't wrestle –'

'Me!' beamed Big Rock. 'Wrestling Troll!'

'But you can't have a match with just one wrestler,' Jack pointed out. 'He needs an opponent.'

'Yes,' nodded Milo. And he looked at Sam.

Sam was silent for a moment, then he sighed heavily and said, 'I could go to jail.'

'Then we rescue you,' said Big Rock.

'That's what I like about Big Rock,' said Milo. 'He always sees everything so simply.'

Milo and Jack followed the directions from Sam, walking through main streets and side streets, until they came to the foot of a tall stone tower.

'There it is,' said Milo.

Jack nodded towards the six armed soldiers, each carrying a long spear and a sword, who took turns patrolling in front of the entrance to the tower, always leaving one soldier standing guard right in front of the door.

'Six against two,' said Jack. 'That's not good odds.'

'Do you think you could turn into Thud?' asked Milo hopefully. 'That would do the trick.'

'I don't know,' said Jack. 'When it happened before, I got this tickly sensation, and my eyes went sort of misty, like I was looking through very thick glass.'

'Any tickly feelings at the moment?' asked Milo.

'No,' said Jack.

Milo sighed.

'Maybe it'll happen once we go into action,' he said.

'Hopefully it won't come to that,' said Jack. 'Once they hear there's wrestling going on in the town centre, they're bound to rush off.'

'Say they don't?' asked Milo, concerned.

In the town square, Big Rock and Sam stood, sizing one another up.

'Proper wrestling rules,' said Big Rock. 'No cheating.'

'I never cheat,' said Sam indignantly.

Robin looked around the town square. It was empty. The horse guessed that most people had seen these two large characters standing opposite one another, flexing their arms and legs as they prepared to fight, and said that

dreaded word 'wrestlers' to themselves, and then hurried indoors, desperate to make sure they didn't get into trouble.

'You'd better get started,' said Robin. 'We need to get those armed guards away from that tower, so Milo and Jack can get in.'

'Good,' nodded Big Rock, and he shuffled towards Sam, then reached out and put his big hand on his shoulder.

Immediately, Sam grabbed Big Rock by the wrist and threw him over his shoulder, to crash into the cobbles.

Big Rock pushed himself to his feet, and shook his head. Then he smiled. 'Good wrestling,' he beamed.

Chapter 5

Milo and Jack watched from the cover of an alleyway as the soldiers continued marching backwards and forwards in front of the entrance to the tower. Milo strained his ears for any sounds of shouting or commotion from the direction of the town square.

'Maybe Big Rock and Sam haven't started wrestling yet,' he murmured.

'Or maybe everyone's too scared to go out and watch them,' suggested Jack.

Milo nodded. 'I think you might be right,' he said. He took a deep breath. 'So it's up to us!'

'You mean we're going to go over there and attack those soldiers?' said Jack, horrified.

'Don't be silly!' said Milo. 'We're going to sneak to them!'

Milo left the cover of the alleyway and ran over towards the entrance to the tower, Jack close on his heels. Immediately, the soldiers turned towards them, the points of their spears aimed at their chests.

'Halt!' cried one. 'Who goes there?'

'There's wrestling going on!' yelled Milo, and he pointed towards the town square. 'Two big men! Actually wrestling! In broad daylight, and in public!'

'Wrestling!' said one of the soldiers, shocked. Immediately, he turned to the others. 'You four, come with me!' He pointed at the remaining soldier. 'You, stay here on guard.'

'Yes, sir!' said the soldier.

The five soldiers ran off towards the town square, and the soldier left behind leapt smartly to attention. Jack noticed a big bunch of keys hanging from the soldier's belt, and gestured towards them to Milo. Milo nodded, then turned to the soldier.

'A terrible thing, wrestling,' he said.

'A crime!' agreed the soldier.

'All those tricky moves,' nodded Milo. 'Especially in tag wrestling. Have you ever seen tag wrestling?'

'Wrestling is a crime!' snapped the soldier. 'Watching wrestling is a crime!'

'I know,' nodded Milo. 'Especially tag wrestling. It's one of the biggest crimes there is. It's when two wrestlers are in the same team, and they work together. Like, say, one of them drops to his hands and knees behind an opponent.'

As Milo said this, Jack dropped to his hands and knees immediately behind the soldier.

'And then the other one pushes the opponent.'

And, as Milo said this, he pushed the soldier, who was so startled he didn't have time to recover and fell backwards over the kneeling Jack and landed flat on his back on the ground. Immediately, Milo hurled himself onto the soldier, holding him down on the ground in a pinfall.

'Grab his keys!' yelled Milo.

Jack snatched the keys from the guard's belt and ran up the stone stairs as fast as he could, heading for the prison cell at the top of the tower. Behind him, he could hear the soldier shouting and thrashing about, but Milo was holding him firmly down.

Jack reached the top landing of the tower and found one door there. He fumbled with the keys, trying different ones that didn't fit the lock, all the time urging himself to go quicker. Milo wouldn't be able to hold the soldier for long, he knew, and then he'd raise the alarm!

At last he found a key that worked! He turned the key, opened the cell door, and ran in.

'Princess!' he called.

The next second he felt a powerful thud in his back, which sent him hurtling forwards to fall face first on the hard stone floor. As he lay there, dazed, he heard the sound of running footsteps, and then pain as someone jumped on his back. He was being attacked! There must have been a guard inside the cell.

As Jack heard pounding footsteps rushing towards him again, he rolled over and at the same time swung his right leg, catching his attacker on the shin.

His attacker fell, sprawling. Jack leapt to his feet and went into a wrestling stance, hands in front of him, knees bent ready to deal with the next move.

His attacker sprang up from the floor of the cell, but – to Jack's astonishment – it wasn't a guard, but the small, thin figure of Princess Ava herself. Jack's mouth dropped open, and he moved towards her.

'Princess –' he began.

That was as far as he got. The Princess took a leap towards him, then sprang into the air and kicked out with both her feet in a hard drop kick that struck Jack fully in the chest, sending him staggering backwards. Before Jack could recover, the Princess was on him, grabbing his left wrist and rolling backwards, sending Jack soaring up into the air, then over her head to crash onto the hard floor of the cell.

'No assassin can beat me!' yelled the Princess.

'I'm not –' began Jack, but once again the Princess moved like lightning, this time dropping on Jack with both knees.

'Ow!' said Jack.

A commotion just outside the cell made Jack and the Princess look towards the doorway, just as four armed soldiers rushed in. Milo was being held by two of them. The other two soldiers pointed their spears at Jack and the Princess.

'Stop!' shouted one of them. 'Put your hands up! Move back to the wall!'

Slowly, Jack and the Princess got to their feet and moved towards the wall, their hands held above their heads. Jack's ribs ached from where the Princess's knees had hit him.

The two soldiers holding Milo pushed him towards Jack and the Princess.

'Right,' said the leading soldier. 'You three will stay here until General Pepper decides what to do with you.'

With that, the soldiers backed out of the cell,

and pulled the door shut. Jack heard the key turn in the lock.

'Where were you?' demanded Milo angrily. 'I held the guard down as long as I could, but then those others turned up!'

'She attacked me,' said Jack, pointing an accusing finger at Princess Ava.

The small red-headed girl stood and scowled at the two boys. Seeing her in her long blue dress embroidered with gold and silver threads, it was hard for Jack to think that she was the same fiery wrestler who'd just floored him.

'Attacked you?' echoed Milo, puzzled. He turned to the Princess. 'Why, when we came here to rescue you?'

'I didn't know that!' responded Princess Ava heatedly. 'I've been expecting General Pepper to send an assassin to kill me, so I thought that's who you were.'

Milo turned to Jack.

'But even so, you should have been able to drag her out. She's just a girl.'

'No, she's not,' said Jack ruefully, and he

rubbed his ribs. 'She's a wrestler.'

'A what?'

'I'm a wrestler,' said Princess Ava defiantly. 'And I'd be a good one, too, if I was allowed to wrestle. But I can't because I'm a Princess.' Suddenly she looked very miserable. 'And there's even less chance of me being a wrestler while I'm locked up in here! Or if I'm assassinated!'

'That won't happen!' Milo assured her.

'Why?' demanded the Princess.

'Because . . .' began Milo. Then he stopped.

'Because you're here to rescue me?' the Princess finished for him, sarcastically. 'Well that plan's a bust!'

'Not just us,' said Jack. 'There are more of us!'

'Oh?' said the Princess, brightening. 'Has the resistance movement risen up? How many are there? Hundreds? Thousands?'

'Er . . . two,' said Jack. 'Three, if you count the horse.'

'Two?!'

'Yes, but two very powerful characters,' said Milo. 'Both wrestlers! Big Rock, a Wrestling Troll and Sam Dent! They won't let themselves get caught so easily!'

The sound of the key in the lock made them turn towards the cell door just as it opened and a soldier looked in. He gave them a nasty grin.

'Just thought I'd let you know, your two wrestling pals have been arrested and locked up in the town jail. Oh, and General Pepper says you two are to be executed for treason, for trying to rescue the Princess!'

With that, the cell door was slammed shut, and they heard the key turn in the lock again.

Chapter 6

Big Rock and Sam sat on the stone benches in the town jail. Both looked gloomy.

'No uprising,' sighed Big Rock. 'No people help us.'

Sam gave an even bigger sigh. 'I suppose they were all just too scared,' he admitted. Then he brightened up. 'But if Milo and Jack have been able to free the Princess, then the people will rally round, I'm sure!'

They heard a voice calling, 'Hey!' from outside. It was Robin.

Big Rock and Sam went to the window of the cell and looked out through the iron bars. The old horse was standing there.

'Any news?' asked Sam eagerly. 'Did Milo

and Jack rescue Princess Ava?'

'No,' said Robin. 'They ended up being locked in the tower with her. And they're going to be executed for treason.'

Big Rock let out a groan that was so loud it made the bricks of the walls rattle.

'Can you two break out of there?' asked Robin.

'No,' said Sam. He gripped the iron bars of the cell. 'These bars are set too deep into the wall. We've tried pushing against them but we can't get enough leverage.'

Robin looked at the iron bars of the window thoughtfully. Then he said, 'Wait there,' and trotted off.

Sam sighed. 'Wait there,' he echoed. 'Where does he think we're going to go?'

Inside the room at the top of the tower, Milo paced, his brain working frantically as he tried to come up with a plan to get them out of this spot. Jack sat on the floor and looked at Princess Ava, sitting on the one chair in the room, her face deep in a thoughtful frown.

'I don't understand this,' said Jack. 'We saw you just a week ago at Lord Veto's. You were the special VIP guest at the Orcs versus Trolls Slamdown.'

'And it was when I came back from there that I found my uncle had taken over. He took the opportunity of my being away to declare himself ruler of Weevil, and had me arrested as soon as I got back.'

'Yes, that's what Sam Dent told us,' said Jack. 'But I can't understand how it can all have happened so quickly! In just a week!'

'Fear,' said Milo. 'There's nothing like a load of heavily armed soldiers knocking on doors to frighten people.' He looked hopefully at Jack. 'Maybe if I kicked you, it would make you angry and you'd turn into Thud?' he suggested.

'It didn't work when she kicked me,' said Jack unhappily. 'Or when she threw me over her shoulder.' He turned to Princess Ava and said, 'You are a very good wrestler.'

'I know I am but, let's face it, you're rubbish,' said Princess Ava. 'You couldn't wrestle your way out of a paper bag!'

'That's not fair!' protested Jack. 'You caught me off guard!'

'Well that's one of the things a wrestler has to do,' said Princess Ava. 'Make sure they're not caught off guard.'

There was the sound of a key turning in the lock, and Princess Ava sprang to her feet, ready to attack. The sight of two soldiers pointing their sharp spears at her made her stop.

'If you had the guts to put those weapons down and face me unarmed, I'd show you who's boss!' snapped the Princess angrily.

A short man walked into the cell, dressed in fine clothes embroidered with gold decorations, and with a gold chain hanging around his neck. He had a nasty smile on his face. This had to be General Pepper, realised Jack.

'And if I were stupid, I would let them put their weapons down,' smirked General Pepper. 'But, as it is, I'm not stupid, and I'm also the boss.'

137

'Nor for long!' growled Princess Ava. 'I am the royal Princess, you are just a general –'

'I'm also your uncle, which means I have royal blood too,' snapped General Pepper. 'Therefore I have the right to be King.'

'You can't be king while I'm alive!' countered the Princess. 'As soon as I reach the age of fifteen, in two month's time, I shall become Queen!'

'Providing you are still alive then,' said General Pepper. Once more he smiled his nasty smile. 'Which, I have to tell you, looks highly unlikely. Once your two friends here have been executed, you will also be executed for treason.'

'You can't execute the Princess!' said Jack, horrified.

'Oh yes I can,' said General Pepper. 'In fact, I've set the date for all your executions as tomorrow. That should stop anyone else from thinking they can rise up in revolution.' He smiled again. 'We'll be doing it in the old-fashioned way: public beheadings in the town square. I do like to keep up the old traditions.'

With that, General Pepper turned and swept out. The two soldiers scowled at Milo, Jack and the Princess and followed General Pepper out of the room, and then the three prisoners heard the key turn in the lock once more.

Chapter 7

Inside their cell, Big Rock and Sam were feeling gloomier than ever.

'I can't see what a horse can do,' groaned Sam.

A whinnying noise outside in the street made them get up.

'That sound like Robin,' said Big Rock.

They both went to the cell window and looked out through the bars. Robin was standing just outside, a long length of chain in his mouth.

'What?' asked Big Rock.

Once more, Robin made a whinnying sound.

'I think he wants us to take the chain from him,' said Sam.

Sam reached through the bars, took hold of

the chain and pulled it into the cell. They now saw that the other end of the length of chain was hooked over Robin's bridle.

'Thank you,' said Robin.

'Why you make that whinny noise?' asked Big Rock, puzzled. 'Why not use proper words like you usually do?'

'Because it's very hard to speak when you've got a mouthful of chain,' said Robin impatiently. 'Right, tie the chain round the bars.'

Sam looped the end of the chain round the bars, and then tied it in a tight knot.

'Ready?' asked Robin.

'Ready,' nodded Sam.

Robin turned away from the window and began to run as fast as his old legs could carry him. Suddenly he jerked to a stop as the chain pulled him up short.

'It's not going to work!' said Sam despairingly.

'Shut up!' said Robin tersely. 'I know what I'm doing.'

With that, the horse leaned, pulling the length of chain so that it stretched tight . . . and then

Robin continued to lean, pulling against the chain. Sam and Big Rock heard the bars set into the wall groan and creak as the knotted chain pulled against them. Robin leaned harder, straining and pulling. Gradually the bars began to bend, and then the next second they hurtled out of the cell window in a shower of stones and dried cement, flying through the air to land on the cobbled street outside.

'Right!' said Robin. 'Now to put the next stage of the plan into operation!'

In the tower, Princess Ava watched, frowning, as once again Milo asked Jack how he felt: if there was any sign of misting over his eyes, or a tingling sensation.

'Why are you asking him all these questions?' she demanded. 'Is he ill?' Then, with a note of alarm, she asked: 'Is it catching? Am I going to catch something off him? I don't want to catch a cold! I'm a Princess!'

'No, nothing like that,' Milo assured her hastily. 'It's –'

'It's private,' interrupted Jack firmly, with a warning look at Milo.

Milo hesitated, then he nodded. 'Yes,' he said. 'It's private.'

Princess Ava looked at Jack in horror.

'You mean it's one of those embarrassing illnesses?!' she said. She gave a shudder of disgust. 'Yuk!'

'No, it's nothing like that!' retorted Jack hotly.

'It's –'

'He turns into a troll,' said Milo. 'When he gets angry.'

'It only happened once!' retorted Jack, annoyed.

He turned to Princess Ava and found her staring at him, her mouth open and an expression of shock on her face.

'It's not my fault!' he said defensively. 'And, as far as I know, it's not catching!'

'How old are you?' she asked.

'Why?' asked Jack.

'Because it might be important,' she said.

Jack shrugged. 'I'm ten.' He shrugged. 'But I don't see –'

'When was your birthday?'

'Two weeks ago,' said Jack.

Princess Ava gave a smug smile. 'You're a half-troll!' she announced.

Jack and Milo exchanged puzzled looks. Then they both asked: 'What?'

'A half-troll,' said Princess Ava. 'People who are half-human, half-troll. It usually doesn't show itself until they're about ten years old. My father told me about them. He'd come across one or two on his travels. They're very rare.' She smiled at Jack. 'You should be proud. Half-trolls make fantastic wrestlers!' Then she looked at Jack doubtfully and added: 'Mind, that might not be the case with you. You look a bit weedy. And you were useless when I fought you.'

'Yes, but when he's Thud he's fantastic!'

The Princess frowned. 'Thud?' she said.

'That's what we call him when he turns into a troll.'

'It's only happened once!' snapped Jack angrily.

But before Jack could say any more, they heard the cell door being unlocked, and then Captain Oz marched into the room, accompanied by about a dozen armed soldiers.

'Prisoners!' he barked at them. 'I have orders to take you at once to the town square, where you will be executed.'

Milo, Jack and Princess Ava stared at Captain Oz in shock.

'Hang on a minute!' said Milo, horrified. 'General Pepper said we're to be executed tomorrow! Not today!'

'General Pepper's changed his mind,' said Captain Oz. Turning to one of the soldiers, he ordered: 'Put the chains on them.'

Chapter 8

Big Rock, Sam and Robin stood in the cover of an alley, by the deserted former wrestling hall, and looked out at the town square. A large crowd of townsfolk had assembled, all of them obviously very anxious, and Sam noticed they kept casting worried looks at the armed soldiers around them.

In the centre of the town square was a large wooden chopping block, and standing next to it was a tall muscular man wearing a black hood and holding a large axe, and a smaller man dressed in heavily decorated clothes and wearing a gold chain.

Suddenly there was a commotion at one side of the square and as Sam, Big Rock and Robin watched, they saw a party of soldiers push their way through the crowd. With the soldiers came Milo, Jack and Princess Ava, all of them with chains wrapped around them, pinning their arms to their sides. They came to a stop by the executioner and General Pepper.

'You said this would happen tomorrow!' said Milo accusingly.

'That was before I got word of your friends escaping,' said General Pepper.

'Escaping?' asked Jack.

'Yes. It seems they broke out of the jail. With two dangerous people like that on the loose, I can't afford to take the risk they might come back with more of their kind and try to free you. This way, they won't have time to put together an army.'

'We don't have an army!' protested Milo. 'There's just us! We're harmless!'

'That,' spat General Pepper, 'is what they all say!' He turned to Captain Oz. 'Execute them. Start with him.' General Pepper pointed a finger at Jack.

'But we're innocent!' protested Jack as the soldiers grabbed hold of him and pushed him towards the execution block. 'We haven't done anything wrong!'

'You've broken the law!' snapped General Pepper. 'And for that you shall be punished!'

Sam, Big Rock and Robin tensed as they watched Jack being forced to his knees and his

head placed on the wooden execution block.

'What are we going to do?' asked Sam desperately.

'We go out there and punch people,' said Big Rock. And he moved out of the alleyway to the back of the crowd.

'It doesn't sound much of a plan,' said Sam.

'You got a better idea?' asked Robin.

'No,' admitted Sam. 'It's just that I don't think we're going to get near enough to stop it before that executioner starts swinging his axe.'

Even as he said it, they saw the executioner lifting his axe into the air, the sunlight glinting on the sharp blade. The soldiers were holding Jack down firmly so that he couldn't move.

'Let's go,' said Robin, and he moved out of the alley, gathering speed as he followed Big Rock at the back of the crowd.

'Here we go!' muttered Sam, and he ran after the horse.

'Leave him alone!' yelled Princess Ava, and she struggled frantically, trying to break free from the soldiers who were holding her, but with their fierce grip and the weight of the chains on her, escape was impossible.

Bent over the execution block, Jack gritted his teeth, ready for the axe to fall.

I won't let them see I'm scared! he vowed to himself. Even though I am! I'm not going to cry!

But even as he thought it, his eyes began to fill up with tears. No, not with tears, with a sort of . . . mist. Like thick opaque crystals forming. And, at the same time, he felt a shuddering sensation course through him.

The executioner had his axe raised to the highest point and was just about to bring it down hard on the boy when he realised that something was happening in front of him. The boy was getting up. No, not getting up, he was growing . . . and changing . . . and getting up.

As the executioner watched, goggle-eyed, a huge creature stood up from where the boy had been kneeling. The two soldiers who'd been holding the boy down were now dangling off the creature, their feet kicking the air. The chains around what had been the boy bulged and stretched, and then snapped and broke as the creature became even wider and taller.

'Yes!' yelled Milo exultantly. 'Thud is here!!'

'Wow!' said Princess Ava, awed.

General Pepper stared upwards at the towering figure of Thud, his mouth open, stunned. Then he snapped out of his shock and yelled out, 'Kill it! Kill the troll! Kill all

of them!'

The executioner also came out of his state of shock and began to swing the axe towards Thud, but the huge creature grabbed hold of the axe by the handle and tore it from the executioner's grasp.

Thud gave a snarl and slammed the axe down hard onto the wooden block, smashing both the axe and the block. Then he reached out and grabbed hold of the shocked Captain Oz, lifted him clear off the ground, and threw him into a group of shocked soldiers, knocking them all down.

'Get us out of these chains!' yelled Princess Ava, as she kicked out at the soldiers nearest to her.

'Happy to oblige!' said a voice.

Milo and Ava turned and saw Sam appear beside them. They looked out into the crowd and saw there was even greater commotion going on as Big Rock grabbed the soldiers nearest to him, and other soldiers dropped to the ground as Robin charged into them.

'Long live Princess Ava!' came a sudden shout from the crowd. And then they heard other voices taking the call up so that it became a chant: 'Princess Ava! Princess Ava!'

Milo became aware that some of the crowd had now also turned on the soldiers. Desperately, the soldiers tried to defend themselves, but as their spears and swords were snatched away from them, many of the soldiers turned and ran.

Meanwhile, Thud was causing havoc, picking up the terrified soldiers and slamming them down on the ground where they lay stunned and senseless.

'Where's General Pepper?' called Milo, searching the crowds, but Pepper seemed to have vanished, lost in the masses. Then suddenly Milo saw him, plucked out of the crowd and held aloft in one of Big Rock's huge fists.

'Here he is!' called Big Rock.

The troll whirled General Pepper around his head, then released him to sail through the air. Thud reached up and skilfully caught the horrified General Pepper, turned him upside down, slammed him to the ground and then fell on him, pinning him down.

'Tag wrestling!' grinned Milo. 'I love it!'

Chapter 9

Within minutes it was all over. General Pepper and Captain Oz were sprawled on the ground, chained together, both looking dazed and bruised. The soldiers who hadn't thrown away their weapons and run were now also sitting on the ground in chains, prisoners.

Big Rock had lifted the Princess up and placed her on his shoulders, so she could acknowledge the crowd as they cheered her and chanted her name. Milo and Jack stood to one side, next to Robin, and joined in the applause for the Princess.

'I still don't know why it happens,' whispered Jack, once again a small, thin boy.

'Just be thankful it did,' whispered back Milo.

Then, with Ava still riding on Big Rock's shoulders, and Sam leading the cheering crowd, they escorted the Princess through the town to the royal palace. Milo, Jack and Robin brought up the end of the procession, just behind General Pepper and Captain Oz and the captured soldiers, who were all loaded down with chains and looking very miserable.

It took another hour for the procession to

reach the palace because so many of the crowd wanted to shake Princess Ava's hand, or bow to her. All of them were also eager to shake the hands of Milo, Big Rock, Sam and Jack . . . although it was obvious that mostly they were very nervous and wary of getting too close to Jack.

When they at last reached the royal palace, Milo noticed that nearly everyone gave Robin an affectionate pat just before they left to go back to their homes.

'Idiots!' grumbled Robin half under his breath, but Milo was sure that the old horse was secretly pleased with the attention he was getting.

Big Rock put the Princess down, and she swept majestically in through the doors of the palace, followed by Sam Dent, Big Rock, the captives, and Milo, Jack and Robin. Once the doors had shut, she turned to her rescuers and said with a sigh of relief, 'I'm glad that's over!'

'What are we going to do with this lot?' asked Milo, gesturing at General Pepper and Captain Oz, and the unhappy chained-up soldiers.

'They're too dangerous to be left walking around free,' added Sam.

'I'm not dangerous!' called out Captain Oz. 'I pledge my allegiance to Princess Ava!'

General Pepper turned and glared at the Captain. 'Traitor!' he spat at him.

'I shall send a messenger to my cousin Edward,' Princess Ava decided. 'He's king of the next kingdom. He never liked Uncle Pepper; he always warned me about him as being sneaky and treacherous.' She looked at the scowling General Pepper. 'I'm sure that King Edward will be pleased to come and take these traitors away and put them in prison, and make them work hard!' She turned to Big Rock and said, 'Will you take them downstairs for me, Big Rock? There's a very damp dungeon down there. They can wait there until King Edward sends his people to collect them.'

'Good,' said Big Rock. And he ushered the chained-up villains towards the stone steps and the dungeons below.

The Princess turned to Jack. 'Also, I take back

what I said before about you being rubbish! You are awesome when you're . . . the wrestling you.'

'Thud,' said Milo. 'His name is Thud.'

'Jack,' corrected Jack. 'My name is Jack.'

'Well, Jack Thud, it was brilliant to see you in action. I owe you my life.' She turned to Milo, Sam and Robin. 'I owe my life to all of you! And I won't forget it.'

Big Rock returned.

'Bad people locked in dungeon,' he announced.

'Good,' said Princess Ava. 'And now, I'd like you all to follow me.'

Chapter 10

As Princess Ava headed towards the grand staircase and began to go up it, Jack and Milo gave each other puzzled looks.

'What's going on?' whispered Jack.

'No idea,' said Milo. He turned to Sam who shrugged, equally puzzled.

They followed the Princess up the stairs to the landing, and joined her by a door she had just opened.

'There!' she said proudly.

They walked into the room, then all stopped and stared, stunned.

The room was the biggest Jack had ever seen – even bigger than the largest rooms in Veto Castle. It looked like a ballroom, except for the rows of seats around all four of the walls, facing inwards. And, there, in the very centre of the huge room . . .

'It's a wrestling ring!' breathed Milo, awed.

And it certainly was – one of the most beautifully decorated and ornate wrestling rings that any of the gang had ever seen.

'My father had it built,' said Princess Ava. 'He liked to invite special wrestlers to come to the palace for private bouts.'

'Wow!' said Milo, still awestruck by the sight of the magnificent ring in the middle of the huge room.

'It's wonderful,' said Jack.

'Good place to wrestle,' nodded Big Rock.

'So would you, Big Rock?' asked the Princess.

'Love to,' he nodded.

'Against me,' added the Princess shyly.

They all looked at her in surprise.

'You?' said Milo.

'The thing is, I've always wanted to be a wrestler. But, because I'm a Princess, I'm not allowed to. But it's always been my dream that one day I'd be in the ring with a professional wrestler. And to be in there with a great Wrestling Troll like Big Rock would be the best thing ever!'

'You're certainly good enough,' Jack told her. 'You beat me.'

Big Rock lumbered towards the ring, and the Princess gave a shout of delight and ran towards it herself.

Sam stopped Big Rock and whispered warningly: 'If you hurt her, you'll have me to deal with.'

Big Rock smiled. 'Fun only,' he said. 'No one get hurt.'

163

'I wouldn't be so sure of that,' muttered Jack. 'You'd better watch yourself, Big Rock. She's got a powerful kick on her.'

Jack and Milo took their seats at the ringside as Big Rock and the Princess climbed through the ropes into the ring. Robin sat down on the floor beside them.

Big Rock and the Princess circled each other. Suddenly the Princess leapt up into the air, aiming herself at Big Rock, and did a drop kick. Both her feet slammed hard against the troll's chest before she landed back on the canvas and did an elegant roll and somersault to take her away from Big Rock, in case he fell and landed on her.

'If that had been anyone else but Big Rock, that would have hurt!' murmured Jack.

'She's good,' nodded Milo in agreement.

Even though he was a hard-as-stone troll, the Princess's dropkick had sent Big Rock stumbling backwards a few paces. Now Big Rock went into a crouch, his huge hands and arms out in front of him, ready to fend off the next attack.

This time, the Princess waited in the centre of the ring, crouching low herself, her arms and hands out in front of her. Suddenly Big Rock made his move, running fast towards her with a speed that was surprising in someone whose bulk was so huge, and for one awful moment Jack thought that the Princess was going to be crushed. Instead, as Big Rock reached her, the Princess ducked beneath Big Rock's arms, grabbed his huge thighs with her small hands, and suddenly straightened up. The next second Big Rock was sailing forwards over her head and crashing down behind her.

'A Back Body Drop!' said Jack, awed. 'She did a Back Body Drop on Big Rock!'

Big Rock and the Princess carried on trading moves and holds and throws. The two had been in the ring for about five minutes, each giving the other as good as they could, when the Princess suddenly ran towards Big Rock, jumped up, put one foot on one of his rocky knees, and then leapt up so that she had her arms around his head. She then threw herself backwards, her arms still around Big Rock's head, dragging the troll forwards at speed. As the Princess landed on the mat in a sitting position, she still held onto Big Rock's head, and he hit the canvas with his face.

'A Bulldog!' grinned Jack.

As Big Rock lay on the canvas, Princess Ava suddenly gave a huge heave with her feet and arms, rolled the big troll onto his back, and then leapt on him, pinning his shoulders to the canvas.

'One! Two! Three!' counted Sam.

The Princess rolled off the troll and sprang to her feet. Sam grabbed her hand and held it aloft. 'I declare the winner to be: Princess Ava!'

Milo and Jack applauded and cheered. As Big Rock got to his feet, the Princess scowled at him. 'You let me win,' she said accusingly.

'Yes,' agreed Big Rock. 'It only fair. Me troll. You human. But you good wrestler.'

'Yes you are,' said Milo as he came to the ring with Jack. 'It's a pity you can't go into the ring and let everyone see how good you are.'

'I wish I could,' said the Princess sadly, 'but it wouldn't fit with me being Queen.' Then she said thoughtfully: 'But perhaps, sometimes, I could take a trip to another country where a wrestling tournament's going on, and where my friends are part of the bill. And maybe I could join them.'

'People would recognise you,' said Jack. 'Word would get back to Weevil.'

'Not if she wore a mask,' said Robin.

Everyone turned to look at the old horse in stunned awe.

'That is a brilliant idea!' said Sam.

Princess Ava smiled. 'Yes!' she said. 'I could be the Masked Avenger! And the only way anyone could get to take my mask off was if they beat me in a match!'

'The Masked Avenger!' smiled Big Rock, impressed. 'Brilliant!'

'Until then, I've got to be a Princess and get my country back together again,' said Ava. 'One of the first things I'll be doing is passing a law allowing wrestling back! And, to organise that,

I appoint Sam Dent, the greatest wrestler ever to come from this kingdom.' She turned to Sam and said, 'You'd better kneel.'

'Why?' asked Sam, puzzled.

'Because it's traditional when giving out a knighthood.'

Sam stared at her, stunned. Then a smile spread over his face. 'Wrestlers don't kneel,' he said. 'Not unless they lose a contest.'

With the same speed and swiftness she'd

shown in the ring with Big Rock, Princess Ava dropped and swung out a leg, catching Sam just below the knee and making him fall. Then just as quickly, she bounced back to her feet as Sam was about to push himself up, but instead he found himself caught in a headlock by the Princess and forced back down to his knees.

'Submit?' she asked.

'I kneel,' grinned Sam.

Princess Ava released her grip from around his head and stepped back. 'Arise, Sir Sam Dent,' she said.

Sam got up, and forced a rueful grin at Big Rock, Milo, Jack and Robin.

'I could have taken her,' he said defensively. 'But she is my future Queen.'

'Oh yes, like we believe you!' said Robin, rolling his eyes.

Chapter 11

The old caravan moved slowly along the country road, heading away from the small town of Weevil. As before, Milo and Jack sat in the driving seat. Once again, Big Rock, the Wrestling Troll, ran around the caravan, all the time throwing punches at the empty air.

'We go back soon?' he asked.

'Soon-ish,' nodded Milo. 'We need to give Princess Ava and Sam time to get the wrestling up and running properly again.'

'Sir Sam,' corrected Jack.

Milo grinned. 'Sir Sam,' he said.

'Ridiculous!' snorted Robin. 'Whoever heard of a wrestler getting a knighthood? Next thing, they'll be giving them out to people like . . .

well, actors and singers.' He snorted again. 'Ridiculous!'

'Anyway, thanks to Princess Ava, at least I know why I turn into Thud,' said Jack. He shook his head. 'I'm a half-troll, and I never knew it!'

'Did she mention anything about how to control it?' asked Milo.

'No,' said Jack. 'She just said that's one of the problems with being a half-troll: learning to control it. She said if I can, it would be fantastic.'

'It certainly would,' said Milo. 'Being able to turn into a troll when you want to, not when your inner troll takes over when you get angry or upset. Now that would be brilliant for wrestling!'

'Yes,' sighed Jack. 'But how do I learn to control it?'

'That's what we've got to find out,' said Milo. 'And we will!'

Suddenly Jack and Milo were aware of a curious sound, low at first, but now getting stronger, almost melodic. And then Jack realised what it was. Robin was singing!

Jack looked at Milo and grinned. And then both joined in with the old horse as he plodded along, hauling the caravan. And soon Big Rock had joined in as well, and the fields and mountains and rivers echoed to the sound of their song:

> 'Wrestling Trolls
> 'Tum-di-dum!
> 'Wrestling Trolls
> 'Tum-di-dum!'

Get ready for more adventures with the Wrestling Trolls in

MATCH 2 HUNK and THUD

Jack is doing fantastically well as the Wrestling Trolls training coach, Big Rock is winning matches, and the group are on their way to more gold and tasty rocks than they can count. All Jack has to do is keep his alter-ego THUD! under control...

Read on for a sneak peek of
HUNK and THUD!

The venue for the Riverdam Slam was absolutely packed. Some of the crowd had dressed up as their favourite wrestlers.

There were at least ten people wearing costumes made to look like Big Rock's multi-patched one, with a picture of a mountain top on the front. About six had come dressed as the wrestler Sam Dent; four girls had dressed up as Grit, the new rising girl-troll star; and two people had perched one on top of the other inside a large sack that had 'Ug the Giant' written on it.

There were at least eight people dressed as

Orcs, complete with fake talons and with red eyeshadow painted around their eyes.

One person was wearing a full-face hood in honour of the Masked Avenger. No one was dressed as Hunk, but Jack guessed that was because Hunk the Half-Troll was a new face on the scene, and no one knew enough about him yet.

The hall lights began to dim, and the harsh bright lights above the ring came on. Into the ring stepped the Master of Ceremonies, wearing a brightly coloured waistcoat and a big yellow bow tie.

'My lords, ladies and gentlemen!' he boomed, his voice filling the hall. 'Welcome to the fantastic Riverdam Slam, featuring some of the greatest wrestlers on the scene today, as well as introducing some of the newest and up and coming wrestling stars of the future!'

At this, the crowd erupted into cheers and stamped their feet and whistled, subsiding as the Master of Ceremonies waved his hands to ask for quiet.

As an expectant hush settled over the crowd, the Master of Ceremonies once again beamed at them and made his announcement, but this time his voice had an apologetic tone.

'Today's programme was due to begin with a contest between Hunk the Half-Troll and Ug the Giant,' he announced. 'But, unfortunately, Ug was taken ill with stomach ache not long ago, and he's had to withdraw.'

'Stomach ache?' queried Milo, puzzled over the news about Ug. 'That's unusual. Most of the giants I've met could eat anything without suffering stomach ache.'

Jack looked around and saw Hunk standing at the back of another section of the hall, his attention fully on the ring in the middle of the hall. If he was disappointed at not being able to take part in the event, he didn't look it.

The crowd shouted out its disappointment, but before things could get out of hand the Master of Ceremonies flashed a big smile and boomed into the microphone, drowning out any unhappy noises. 'So instead we move to the next bout on the bill. A brilliant young rising star of Troll Wrestling, the truly formidable, and so far unbeaten . . . my lords, ladies and gentlemen, I give you . . . Grit!'

With that, the curtain at the back of the hall opened and the small, stocky figure of Grit appeared. Her wrestling costume of brightly multi-coloured spangles twinkled and shone, matching the crystalline of her rocky and stony skin.

Grit waved at the crowd, who cheered the small troll loudly as she stomped down the aisle to the ring, and pulled herself into it through the ropes.

While Grit stood in one corner of the ring and waited, the MC took centre stage again.

'And now, Grit's opponent, that mystery wrestler who is known only as the Masked Avenger! Yes, ladies and gentlemen, she wears a mask to hide her identity. Who is she? There will be only ever be one way for her mask to come off and her identity to be known. If she loses, then the person who defeats her has the right to take the mask from her head! Will that be her fate today against Grit?'

At this, there rose a huge cheer from the crowd, along with shouts of, 'Yes!' and 'Take her mask off! Take her mask off!'

'My lords, ladies and gentlemen!' boomed the MC, flinging his arm towards the curtains at the back of the hall. 'Let's have a huge Riverdam Slam welcome for . . . the Masked Avenger!'

The curtains parted and into the hall stepped Jack and Milo's friend, Princess Ava, dressed as the Masked Avenger. Her costume was purple and she wore a hood with two eyeholes in it completely covering her head. The crowd continued chanting, 'Take her mask off! Take her mask off!' as Princess Ava ran down the aisle, somersaulted over the ropes into the ring to land nimbly on her feet, and then did another somersault into the centre of the ring.

It was strange for Jack to see two wrestlers he liked battling each other – but he would always have to root for his friend Princess Ava.

He didn't want her identity to be revealed, ever!

The Masked Avenger saluted the crowd as the MC announced, 'The rules: the first to get two pinfalls or two submissions to a count of three, or a knockout to a count of ten, is the winner. And now, let the action begin!'

The bell by the side of the ring sounded.

The Riverdam Slam was underway!

The Masked Avenger darted out of her corner and threw herself at Grit, her short, stocky girl-troll opponent. Jack winced and half-closed his eyes in anticipation of the Avenger crashing into the solid, rocky figure. Instead the Avenger surprised everyone, including Grit, by suddenly dropping to the canvas seconds before she hit Grit and sliding into the small troll's shins. She grabbed the troll's legs with both hands, and then slid around behind her, pulling back to try and pull the troll over.

It didn't work.

Grit used her weight and her low centre of gravity to remain solidly upright. Then she reached down, grabbed the Avenger by one arm and threw her up into the air, caught her as she came down, and hurled her hard at the nearest corner post.

The Masked Avenger thudded into the post and crashed to the canvas.

'Ouch!' winced Jack. 'That must have hurt.'

'I told you Grit was good,' murmured Milo.

Grit lurched towards the corner, one foot raised to crunch the Avenger beneath it, but the Avenger rolled swiftly away, and Grit's foot stamped down on the canvas, narrowly missing the Avenger.

The Avenger bounced up and leapt backwards as Grit turned and lunged at her. Once again Grit just missed. The Avenger was fast.

The Avenger went on the attack again, this time jumping high and leaping on to Grit's shoulders, her feet gripping Grit's head on either side. Then the Avenger tried a forward roll, but again Grit used her weight and low centre of gravity to stand still, like a rock. Grit slammed her hands up to clap the Avenger's ankles to the sides of her head, and the Avenger found herself upside down with her feet trapped in Grit's rocky fists.

BANG!

Grit slammed the Avenger down head first and then let go of her ankles.

The Avenger, dazed by the double blow to the top of her head, fell down and immediately Grit fell on her, pinning both the Avenger's shoulders to the canvas. Although she struggled hard to lift first one shoulder, then the other, the Avenger was no match for the troll-type weight of Grit.

'One!' shouted the crowd approvingly, as the referee began the count. 'Two! Three!'

Grit pushed herself up off the fallen Avenger and returned to her corner, while the crowd erupted with shouts of, 'Grit! Grit! Grit!' and 'Take her mask off!'

'It's not looking good for Ava,' said Jack, worried. 'It'll finish her wrestling career if she gets unmasked here.'

Find out what happens to Ava in the next instalment of

Wrestling Trolls:

HUNK and THUD

COMING SOON!

Don't miss these other exciting adventures from Hot Key Books ...

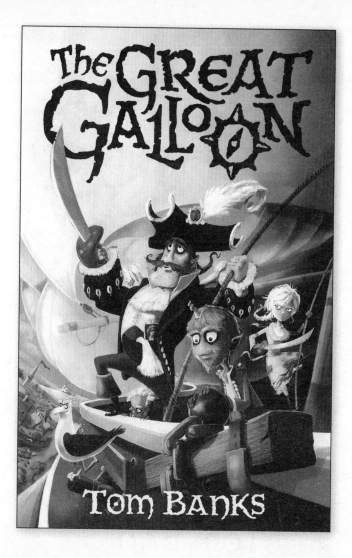

The Great Galloon is an enormous airship, built by
Captain Meredith Anstruther and manned by his
crew, who might seem like a bit of a motley bunch
but who are able to fight off invading marauders
whilst drinking tea and sweeping floors!

Captain Anstruther and his motley crew of
sky-pirates are back for more adventures!

A squirrel, a hot dog stand, the planet Jupiter...
what will get shrunk next?

THE SUNDAY TIMES 'Book of the Week'

SHRUNK!
MAYHEM AND METEORITES

F. R. HITCHCOCK

All is quiet in the sleepy seaside town of Bywater-by-Sea
- that is, until two meteorites fall to earth -
landing in the middle of the Field Craft Troop's
outdoor expedition camp.

Uniquely written by 2000 children and Fleur Hitchcock
in the online live writing project, TheStoryAdventure.com

TROUBLE
WITH MUMMIES

F.R.HITCHCOCK

Probably the first really noticeable thing was Mum coming back from the hairdresser's on Friday afternoon, wearing a small black beard.

HARVEY DREW
AND THE BIN MEN
FROM OUTER SPACE

Harvey Drew is an ordinary eleven-year-old
who dreams of great adventures in outer space.
The Toxic Spew is an intergalactic waste disposal ship.
The two are on a collision course for chaos!

Billy Slipper is a fairly normal boy with a definitely
not-so-fairly normal family. All he wants to do is add
to his 'Collectabillya' (an assortment of weird and
wonderful objects he finds) in peace, but his cleaning-
mad mum (she even clingfilms the carrots!) and his
fantastically horrid twin sister have other ideas.